To Marie–Louise and Michael
M. M.

For my granddaughter, Fiona
Z. C.–L.

What I Like Most

MARY MURPHY

illustrated by **ZHU CHENG-LIANG**

CANDLEWICK PRESS

What I like most in the world is my window.

This morning, through my window,

I see the mailman at the red gate.

I see a blackbird in my tree.

When I breathe on the glass,

I can make drawings that quickly disappear.

My window won't change,

but the things outside will.

Some people will leave the street.
Some new people will come.
The trees will grow, and so will
the children, including me.

WE ARE
MOVING
→

Here at my window,
I can imagine it all.
This window is what
I like most in the world.

Except for apricot jam.

My grandmother makes it in a huge copper pot,
and her house smells of apricots for hours.
She gives everyone a jar.
When our jar is nearly empty,
I put only a tiny bit on my toast to make the jam last.

Apricot jam is what I like most in the world.

Except for these shoes.

They have lights that flash to show where I am going.

I can walk and run and jump in them.

My feet do a tiny bounce with every step.

One day the shoes will wear out,

or my feet will grow too big for them.

Right now they are what I like most in the world.

Except for the river.

Trees grow all along the river.

Fish and ducks live in it, and once I saw an otter.

Today the river is shiny as a mirror.

We sit on the big rock that is like an island.

In winter the river is huge
and races along.
In summer it is shallow,
and we can splash right across it.

The river changes,
but it is always the river.
That is why I like it most
in the world.

Except for this pencil.

It is red outside and red inside.
Its color comes out like a red ribbon.
When you sharpen it, the point gets small and fine
and the pencil gets shorter.
Someday it will be all used up, and it will disappear.

It is what I like most in the world.

Except for fries.

When I smell them cooking,

I get to the table before they do.

I like them best when they are almost too hot.

I dip every fry in the middle of my egg.

When the egg is finished, I dip my fries in ketchup.

Soon my plate is empty.

Fries are what I like most in the world.

Except for this book.

It has a story about someone quite like me.
I know it by heart, but I still want to hear it again.
I can say it in my head and see the pictures.

It is a funny book. It is interesting.
Maybe I won't want to read it every day when I am bigger.

But for now it is what I like most in the world.

Except for this teddy.

When I got him, he was the same size as me.

Now I am bigger than him.

He comes everywhere with me.

He sleeps with me. He is a good friend,
and I will always have him.

He is what I like most in the world.

Except for you.

You have been here since before I was born.

You look after me.

Mostly we have good times.

Even when we are upset with each other,

we belong together.

And even though you change

and I change . . .

you are what I like

the very, very most in the world.